MW00915676

Mirabella & the & Monarch's Magical Migration

Scott Stoll

with Parker Woods Montessori School

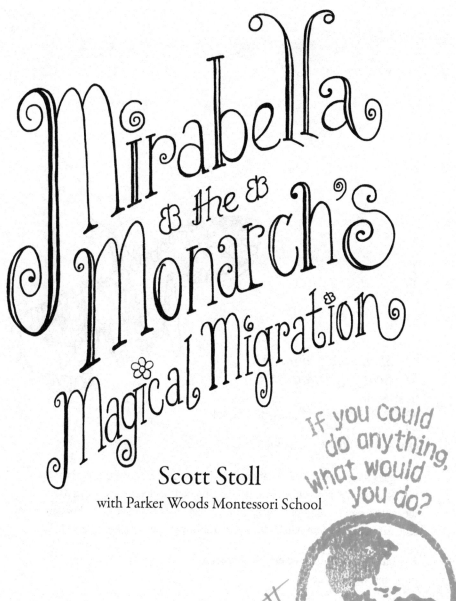

If you could do anything, what would you do?

the Argonauts

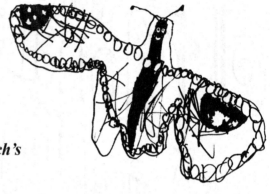

Mirabella the Monarch's Magical Migration

Scott Stoll

with Parker Woods Montessori School

For bulk orders or signed copies contact us:
http://theArgonauts.com

Permissions: Illustrations reproduced courtesy of Parker Woods Montessori Elementary School staff, teachers, parents and students. See acknowledgments pages 93–100. Cover art by Scott as inspired by dozens of students. Back cover photo by Tim Spanagel of Massey Green Aerial Video Photography (MasseyGreenAVP.com) and Scott Stoll with Parker Woods Montessori. Thanks to Judy Ganance for the picture of the caterpillar on the opposite page. For updates to this page, please visit: http://theArgonauts.com/about/copyright#books

Library of Congress Control Number: 2017903455

ISBN: 9780982784266

A thousand monarch butterflies clinging to a branch in the Monarch Butterfly Biosphere Reserve in Mexico.

From Scott's trip around the world on a bicycle.

A monarch caterpillar eating milkweed in the garden at Parker Woods Montessori elementary school.

Photo courtesy of Judy Ganance.

Chapter 1:
A Miraculous Metamorphosis

Parker Woods Montessori

Behind a school.
In the garden.

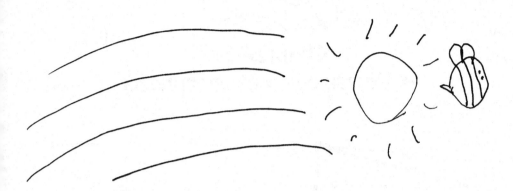

A momma monarch searches for the perfect milkweed plant, tasting each one with her feet. Yes! — with her feet.

Soon, she finds a lush, tasty milkweed plant with strong leaves and roots that change the sun and the minerals locked in the earth into delicious, nutritious butterfly food.

3

The momma monarch butterfly lays
a tiny egg on the bottom of a milkweed
leaf. She whispers an important secret and
finishes by pronouncing, "And so, my little
messenger, I name you —
Esperanza the Fourth."

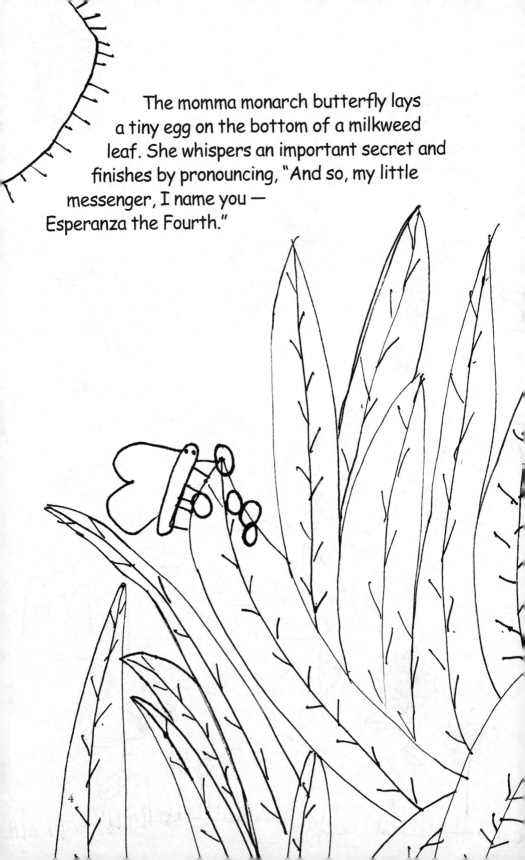

Then she flies away. The momma monarch is very busy. She has to lay hundreds of eggs to create her army of caterpillars. An army is what you call a group of caterpillars, like a pride of lions or a troop of monkeys —

Draw
your
picture
here.

Or a pandemonium of parrots —

Or a kaleidoscope of butterflies.

About four days later Esperanza the Fourth
hatches. She is already in her second stage
of life. Caterpillars are a type of larva like
maggots or grub worms but more cute.

She is only about two millimeters long and translucent (see-through) green so she can hide from predators. But soon she grows bigger and develops yellow, black and white stripes that are a warning to stay away.

Milkweed is poisonous to most birds and mammals, and because the caterpillars eat only milkweed, they are also poisonous. Not to mention, they taste terrible.

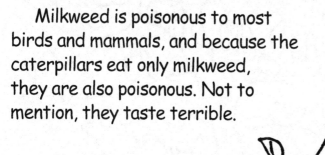

Esperanza has a voracious appetite, meaning she is a very, very hungry caterpillar. In fact, she accidentally ate this page.

But caterpillars don't like paper. The caterpillar's favorite and only food is the milkweed plant. They are very picky eaters, like panda bears who only eat bamboo —

Or koala bears who only
eat eucalyptus —

Or blue whales who only eat krill.

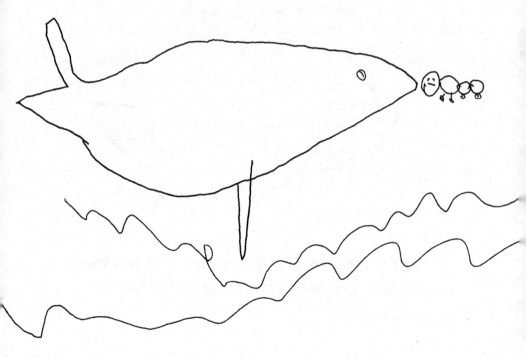

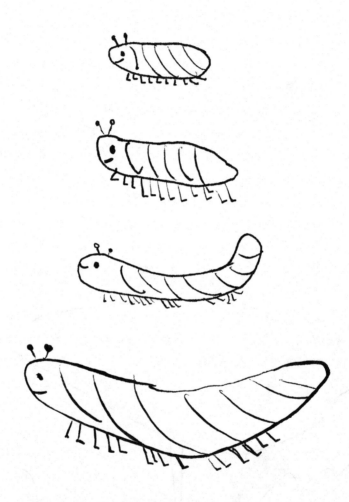

The little caterpillar ate and ate for two weeks continuously and every day grew and grew.

Meanwhile —

Esperanza worries aloud, "I can't wait to grow up and be a beautiful butterfly, but I don't **look** like a butterfly, and I don't **feel** like a butterfly. Maybe I'm not a caterpillar; maybe I'm just a worm."

"Either way you just need to accept yourself, warts and all," says Cutey the Toad. "True beauty is on the inside."

"Aren't I supposed to tell you that?" says Esperanza.

Cutey laughs politely.

Esperanza sees the birds fly by and says, "I wish I could soar like an eagle, but I'm just a worm with legs. I can walk, but I'll never be able to fly."

"You have to learn to crawl before you can walk," says Crawley the Earthworm.

"And you need to learn to run before you can fly," says Blossom the Bird.

"That's very kind of you both, but aren't I supposed to tell you that?" says Esperanza.

Crawley and Blossom laugh politely.

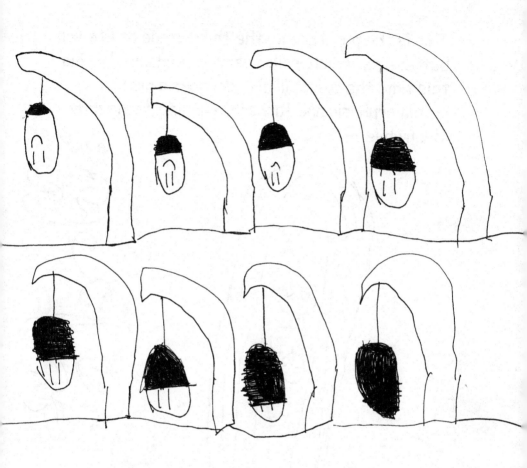

Then one day, despite her worries, nature takes over. The caterpillar grows very sleepy and weaves herself a nice warm place to nap called a chrysalis. "I'll just close my eyes for a little while," Esperanza thinks.

This is the pupal stage, the third stage of life for butterflies, which is like being a teenager. During this time the caterpillar undergoes a magical metamorphosis and turns into an adult butterfly. Meanwhile —

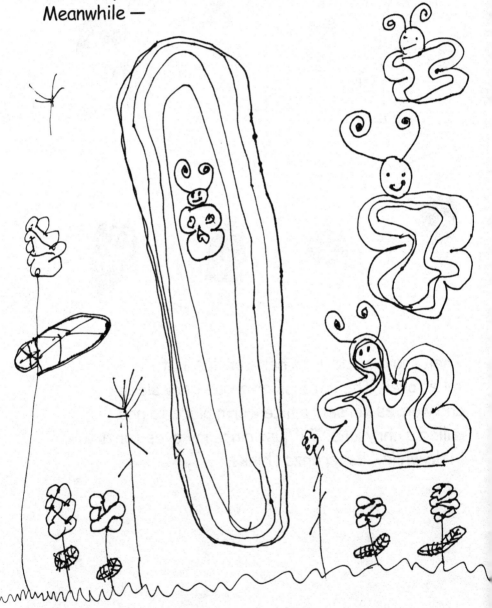

Esperanza dreams of flying all the way around the world and to the ends of the Earth. She'd even like to get in a spaceship and go to the Moon or Jupiter. However, most of all she wants to visit Butterfly Land.

19

Two weeks later Esperanza awakes and is surprised to see that she is a beautiful, regal monarch butterfly, the king of all 24,000 butterfly species, hence **monarch**. Or in this case, the queen of butterflies. And she has an equally impressive scientific name: **Danaus plexippus**. Try saying that five times fast.

From a tiny egg of just 1 millimeter,
Esperanza is now 120 times bigger —
but weighs less than one penny.

21

How the green leaves of the milkweed turn into the yellow, black and white caterpillar that turns into a fiery orange butterfly are just two of the many mysteries of the monarch. You could say it is a kind of magic.

Another mysterious, magical thing is that the caterpillar has 16 legs and the butterfly has only 6 legs! Where did they go?

And the best magical mystery is that adult butterflies have wings. Where did those come from?

"You're such a beautiful lady," says Lily the Ladybug.

Although everyone thinks of Esperanza as a beautiful, smart butterfly, Esperanza doesn't think of herself that way. She's having difficulty adjusting to the sudden change and still feels like a little worm with legs.

"Don't worry," says Bubbles the Bumbling Bumble Bee. "Just **bee** the change you want to see."

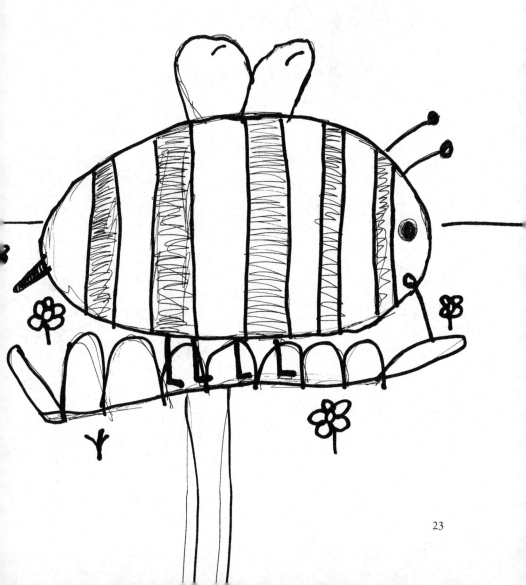

"Nothing's purr-fect," says Snowflake the Kitty. "There's always room for improvement.

"That's very kind of you both, but aren't I supposed to tell you that?" says Esperanza.

Bubbles and Snowflake laugh politely.

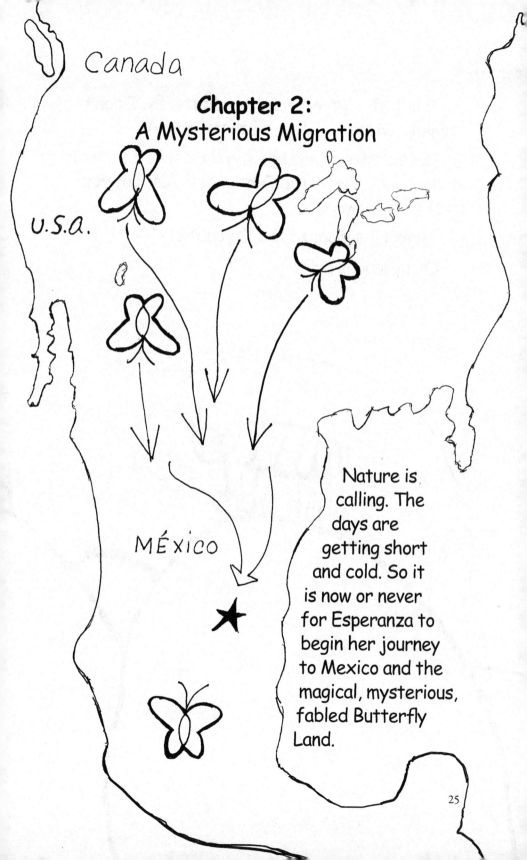

Canada

Chapter 2:
A Mysterious Migration

U.S.A.

MÉXICO

Nature is calling. The days are getting short and cold. So it is now or never for Esperanza to begin her journey to Mexico and the magical, mysterious, fabled Butterfly Land.

"I'm just a little, brand new butterfly. I don't think I can make it," says Esperanza.

"Sometimes all you need to do is take a step of action," says Cenny the Centipede. "Just put your best foot forward."

"Aren't I supposed to tell you that?"

Cenny laughs politely.

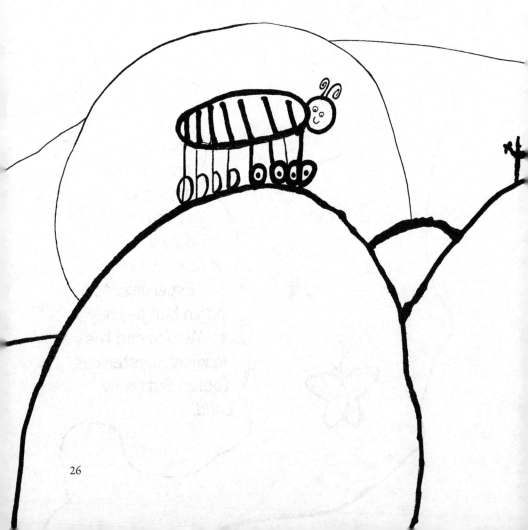

"I'm not sure I can. A few weeks ago, I didn't even have wings," says Esperanza.

"Give it a try. Sometimes you just need to take a leap of faith," says Hopper the Grasshopper.

"Aren't I supposed to tell you that?"

Hopper laughs politely.

So, Esperanza flutters her wings, then flits, then flaps, then flippity flaps. And — to her great surprise — finally flies away.

Another big mystery is how a monarch butterfly knows where anything is and whether to fly north or south or the difference between east and west.

Maybe butterflies just follow the weather. Or maybe they follow the magnetic pull of the earth or the position of the sun.

To Esperanza it is an instinct, which is like having an inner map.

29

However, she still doubts herself. "How will I know how far to go?"

"Keep all eight of your eyes open for opportunity, and you'll know it when you see it," says Waterspout the Spider.

"Aren't I supposed to tell you that?" says Esperanza.

Waterspout laughs politely.

Esperanza has all kinds of adventures.
She flies past a farm. And —

Under bridges, up and over walls, through forests,
between buildings and along roads.

She meets a lot of creatures, like a house fly.
And a house that can fly —

And the strange flutterby —

And butter that can fly.

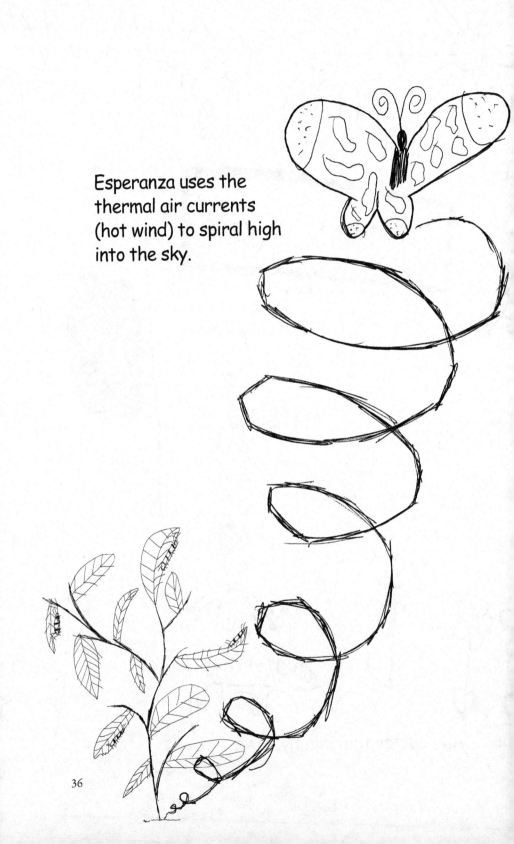

Esperanza uses the
thermal air currents
(hot wind) to spiral high
into the sky.

36

But sometimes she is blown
backwards in strong headwinds —

Or caught in the rain.

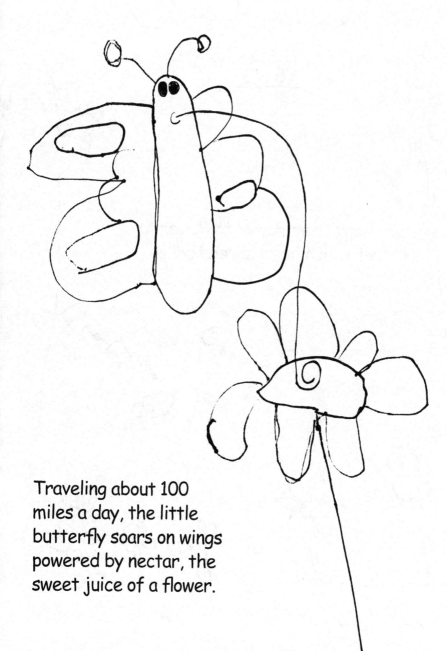

Traveling about 100
miles a day, the little
butterfly soars on wings
powered by nectar, the
sweet juice of a flower.

She hops from flower to flower to refuel, which helps spread pollen.

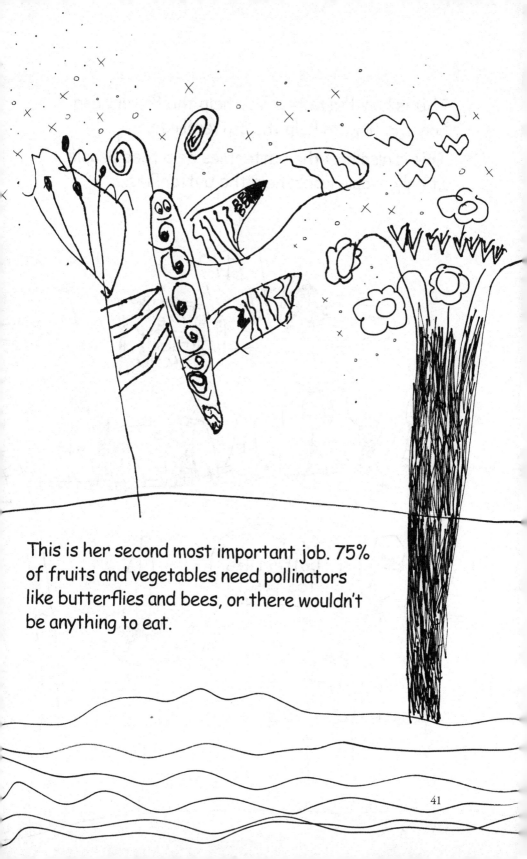

This is her second most important job. 75% of fruits and vegetables need pollinators like butterflies and bees, or there wouldn't be anything to eat.

This is how the butterflies help the flowers and how the flowers help the butterflies.

This is also how the butterflies help feed people. If only people would help the butterflies...

Day after day Esperanza travels,
hiding at night —

And basking in the morning sun
before continuing again.

Esperanza doesn't think she will ever find Butterfly Land. "Don't worry. You'll get there eventually," says Dash the Snail.

"Aren't I supposed to tell you that?" says Esperanza.

Dash laughs politely.

She has to be careful. Even though monarch butterflies are poisonous to most predators, some lizards, frogs and insects can still eat them.

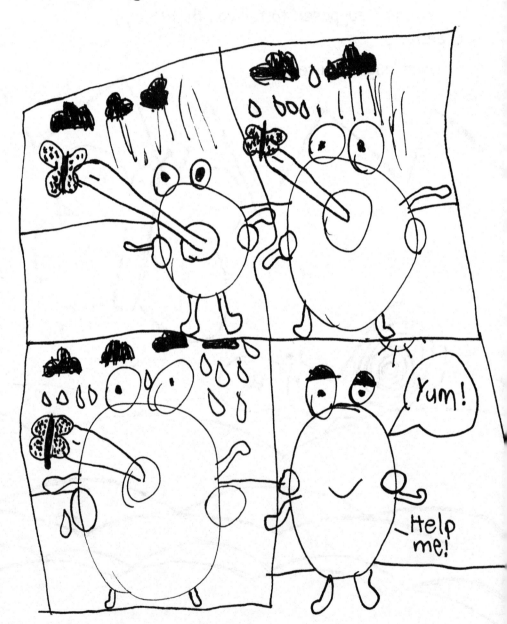

And Black-backed Orioles and Black-headed Grosbeaks birds are the only birds that can eat a monarch without getting sick.

Of course, there are other natural dangers, but the most challenging and dangerous thing is flying over or around cities, and going long stretches through farmlands with nothing but corn and no milkweed, no flowers and no nectar to sip —

And dodging cars (no one taught her to look
left, right and left again) —

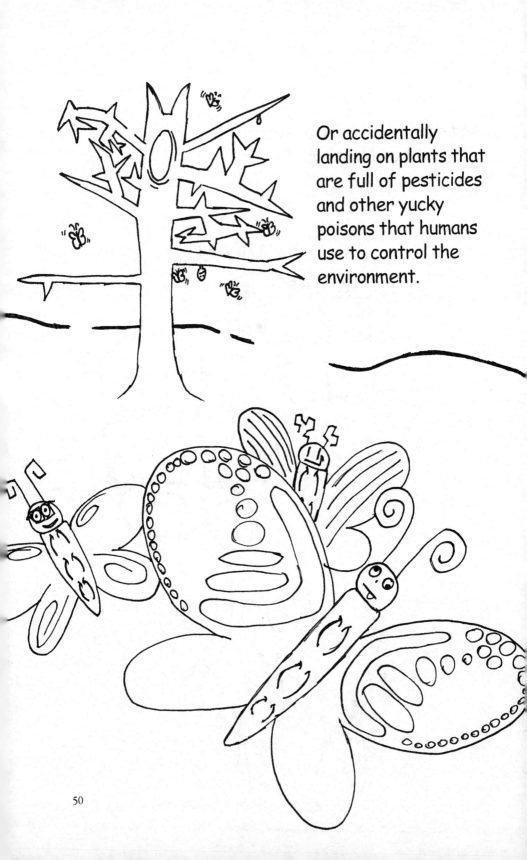

Or accidentally landing on plants that are full of pesticides and other yucky poisons that humans use to control the environment.

"You need to learn the difference between being all bark and no bite and being all bite and no bark," says Cupcake the Dog.

"That's good advice to keep me safe, but aren't I supposed to tell you that?" says Esperanza.

Cupcake laughs politely.

"Oh! I'm never going to make it," says Esperanza the Fourth.

"Slow and steady wins the race," says Tuck the Turtle.

"Aren't I supposed to tell you that?" says Esperanza.

Tuck laughs politely.

"Why are you laughing? Why does everyone keep laughing at me?"

"It just seems funny because another butterfly, just like you, told me, 'Slow and steady wins the race.' And now I'm telling you. What was her name? Esperanza the Second or was it the Second Hundredth?"

7 6 5
8 .4
.3
71 . .70
72 .69 60.59
73 .68 61 .58
74 .67 .57
9 2 75 .62 .56
76 .66 .56
65 63
.1 77 64 .55 53
52
51
50
.49

10 78. .54
96.
79. 95.
80. 94.
11 93.
12 81. 92.
13 82. 91.
14 15 .16 41 42 43 44 45 46
20 19 18 17 83. 90. 40 39 38 37
21 84. 36
85. 89.
.22 86 88 .35
.23 28. 87
24 25 26 27 29. 34
30 31 32 33

.A °F

D °G I N W
°C H• •P •Q
M° •R •X V
•J Z.
°B E. °L •K U
T °S .Y

O.

53

Esperanza kept flying. Through Cincinnati, Ohio.
Past Kentucky.

Past the Mississippi River and
out of the Midwest —

And the Southwest —

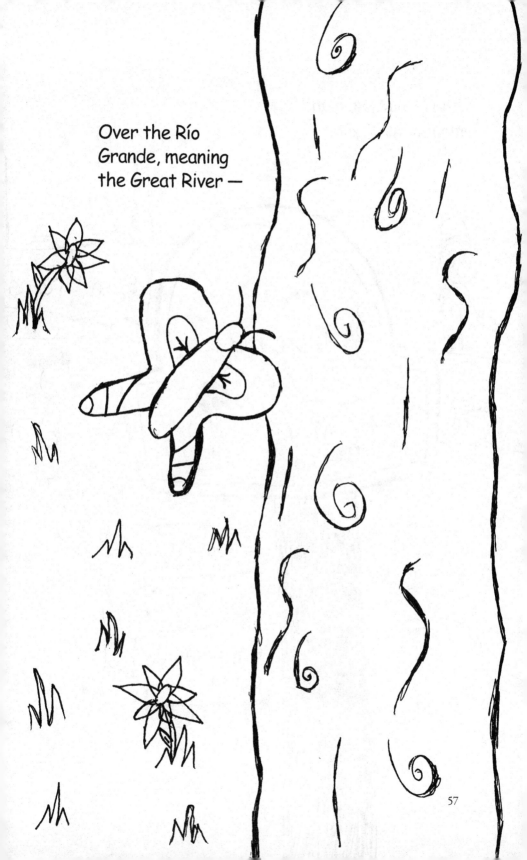

Over the Río
Grande, meaning
the Great River —

And into Mexico and the
mountains beyond.

Soon she sees one monarch.
"Hello! How are you, friend?

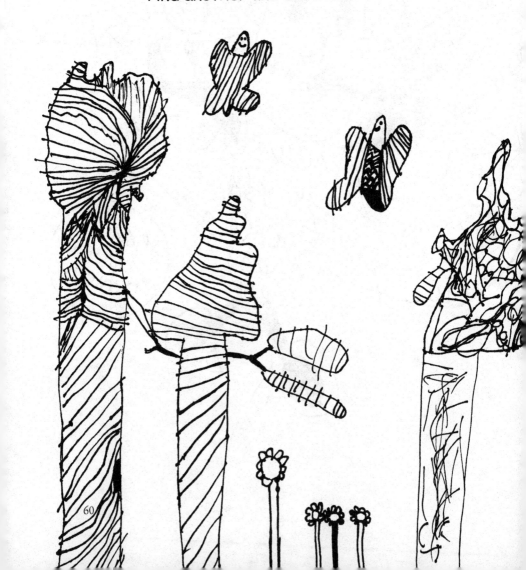

"Fancy meeting you here."
"The fancy is all mine," she says.
And then she sees another monarch.
"Fancy meeting you here."
And another and another...

The further she goes the more monarch
butterflies she sees until soon the blue skies
are on fire with a million butterflies.

Even the evergreen trees aren't green anymore, but orange from all the roosting monarchs. It looks like a forest made of butterflies.

At long last, Esperanza has arrived at **"El Santuario de la Mariposa Monarca."** That is Spanish for "The Monarch Butterfly Sanctuary." It is the fabled Butterfly Land, full of exotic creatures.

Esperanza even finds the very same tree that
her ancestors had made their winter home four
generations ago. The branches are full of so many
butterflies that they droop and sometimes break.

Butterflies are very mysterious and the biggest mystery of all is: What are they doing in Mexico besides hiding from Old Man Winter? The secret is that butterflies migrate to Mexico for their annual meeting to discuss the current state of affairs, and how they can make the world a better place.

And, they agree the
world needs butterflies
more than ever.

"But what can we do to help? There are fewer butterflies now than ever. And no one is paying attention to us," says a butterfly. "We taught them that change is possible, like the caterpillar turning into a butterfly, but that didn't work."

"And we taught them that little things can make a big difference, like how the flapping of a butterfly's wings, like dominoes falling, can cause it to rain far away. But that didn't work," says another.

"And we taught them that nature is as fragile as a butterfly's wings, but that didn't work," says another.

"Nothing is working," they all say at once.

The conversation went on long into the night until Huracán, a very old and wise butterfly who is rumored to be more than twelve generations old, asks Esperanza the Fourth, "Why haven't you had anything to say?"

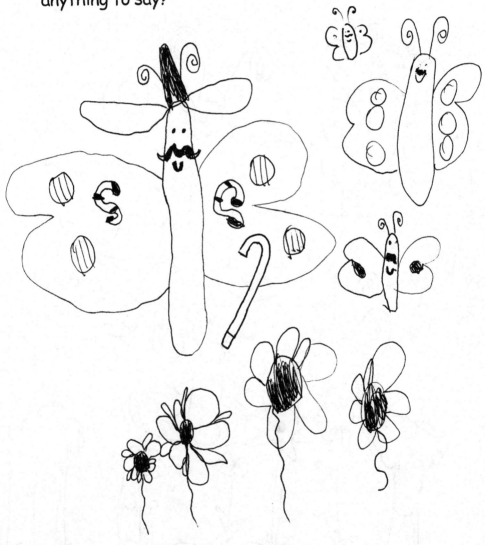

"I'm sorry. I'm not a very good butterfly," says Esperanza. "I tried to spread the message of hope, but instead everyone just kept giving me hope."

This caused a great commotion among all the butterflies. "Sorry, I tried," she says, thinking the butterflies are mad.

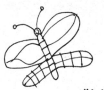

"No. No. That's great news, Esperanza! It means last year's message was a success. Not only did we spread hope but now everyone else is too! You see they gave the hope back to you!"

"Well done, Esperanza!" everyone cheers.

"You see," says Huracán, "We're all in this world together, and one generation learns from the next. And soon our wisdom will be piled high as the tallest mountain. That's the Butterfly Effect: small changes can make big differences. One flap of our wings might bring a hurricane to the Gulf or a long drought to the Midwest. So, imagine if our wings can make such a difference, what kind of difference our words will make!"

Esperanza suddenly understands.

"Oh," she says. "What comes around goes around. It's like magic."

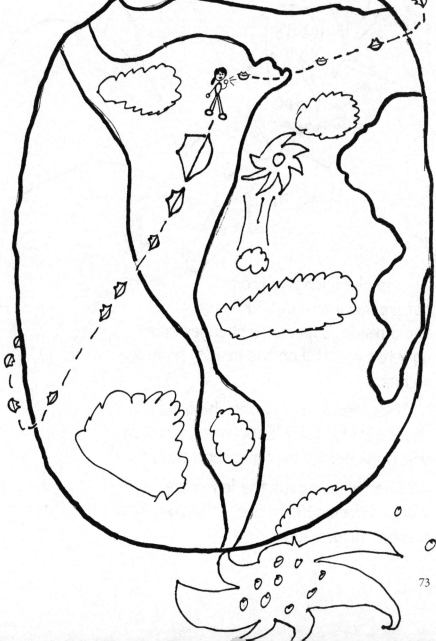

73

And like changing from a
caterpillar into a butterfly on
the outside, Esperanza changes from
ugly to beautiful on the inside, from sad
to happy.

"Now there is only one thing left to
do," says Huracán. "Esperanza, what do
you think next year's message should be?"

She thinks about the lessons she
learned during her travels then makes a
humble suggestion.

The butterflies put Esperanza's idea to a vote
and the decision is a unanimous: "Yes!"

At last peaceful and fulfilled, Esperanza snuggles tight with her new friends to stay warm for the long winter. During the day she studies Spanish; and at night she dreams of all the amazing adventures she had, until she has relived every moment of her great migration with a new understanding.

Then she dreams of flying home to the land
of snowy winters, and raising her own family
and leaving her legacy to the world — her
magical message.

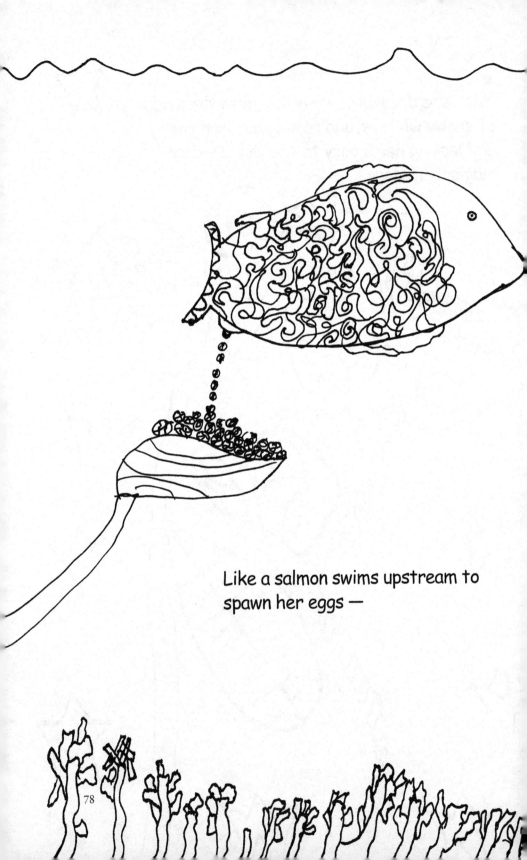

Like a salmon swims upstream to
spawn her eggs —

Or the sea turtle swims across oceans
to their nesting grounds —

Or the wildebeest circles East Africa
for greener pastures —

Or the arctic tern follows summer
halfway around the globe —

When the days get long and warm
again, hundreds of millions of monarch
butterflies begin the long migration
home to where the delicious
milkweed grows.

Along the way, Esperanza finds a mate.

And soon lays her first egg on the bottom of a milkweed plant.

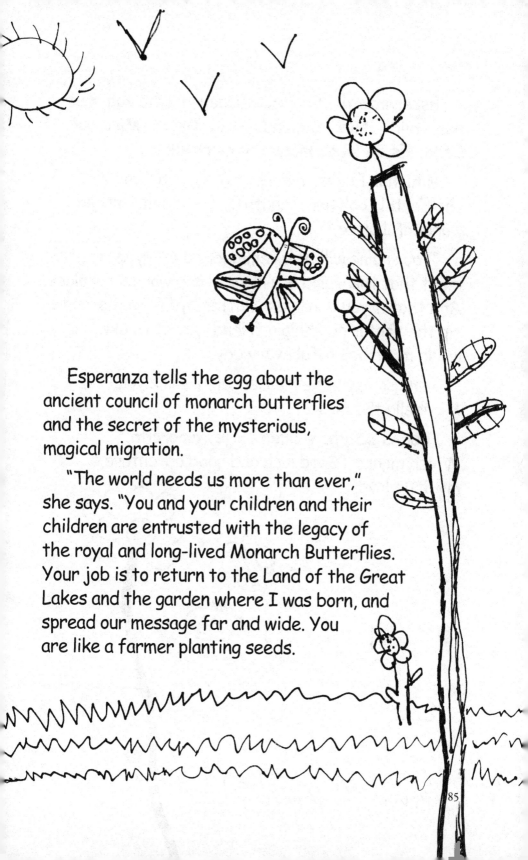

Esperanza tells the egg about the ancient council of monarch butterflies and the secret of the mysterious, magical migration.

"The world needs us more than ever," she says. "You and your children and their children are entrusted with the legacy of the royal and long-lived Monarch Butterflies. Your job is to return to the Land of the Great Lakes and the garden where I was born, and spread our message far and wide. You are like a farmer planting seeds.

Esperanza the Fourth whispers to the egg, her new child: **"¡Mira el mundo — la Tierra! Mira qué bella. Es un lugar mágico y maravilloso."**

Which in English means: "Look at the world — the Earth! Look how beautiful. It is a magical and wonderful place."

"Your name will be a reminder to everyone you meet that the world is a magical and wonderful place. And that if you don't just flutter by life, but stop to sip the nectar and help a friend, you can make the world more beautiful every day."

"And so, my little messenger, I name you — Mirabella the First."

"Buena suerte y buen viaje, amorcito." Which means: "Good luck and good adventure, my little love."

The beginning

Add
your
caption
here.

Challenges

Complete 12 out of the 18 challenges below to win the
butterfly trophy and bragging rights.

❏   Color your favorite picture.

❏   Read this book to a friend.

❏   How many butterflies are in this book?

_____

❏   Draw your picture on page 5.

❏   Complete the connect the dot drawing on page 53.

❏   Add your caption on page 89.

❏   If Mirabella's message is that we can make the world
an even more beautiful place, what was Esperanza's
message? Hint: What does her name mean in Spanish?

_____

❏   What was the message during Huracán's generation?

_____

❏   If you could deliver an inspirational message to
everyone you meet, what would it be?

_____

❏   Find a mistake.

_____

❏   Look up a new word in a dictionary.

_____

☐ Find 10 things or characters in the book listed on page 96 in the acknowledgments.

☐ Find 2 signs to Mexico.

☐ Find Scott riding his bicycle around the world, and Furrell his lost black cat.

☐ Visit our website to learn how to save the butterflies: http://theArgonauts.com/save-the-butterflies/

☐ What do honeybees have in common with butterflies?

_____

☐ Plant a butterfly garden with milkweed and other native plants and flowers.

☐ How would you like to help the butterflies?

_____

_____

_____

91

About the Project

We hope you enjoyed our book because we all love monarch butterflies. Like many species on our planet, monarchs face many challenges. The population has shrunk dramatically, and their great migration has nearly collapsed more than once. This was a difficult story to write because I wanted to help, but I didn't want the story to be depressing or preachy. Eventually, I chose to focus on the inspirational qualities of the monarch migration as an example of how we can make the world a better place.

It continues to be an honor to work with the schools. The young students always add more to what I imagine possible. Not all principals are willing to accept additional responsibilities especially real-world projects, so the kids are lucky to have Ms Simmons. And, not all schools have art teachers; so these students are double lucky to have Suzanne Nall as their art teacher. (Her influence is apparent in these drawings. You won't just see the subject matter floating in white space, but complete environments with overlap, perspective and tiny details. I encourage you to look closely. Almost every object, even if unrecognizable, has a purpose for being in the drawing.) We also had a lot of side projects, many arranged by the dedicated PTO, including Nuria López, who brought the project to the school, and Judy Ganache who organizes the certified Monarch Way Station (see her picture on page V). Here are a few project highlights:

- Students raised, tagged and released monarchs for the long flight to Mexico.
- The Glow Show art exhibit: a bigger-than-life, blacklight, papier-mâché, butterfly garden.
- March Reading Madness and Science Fair, both featuring butterflies.
- A milkweed seed giveaway so the kids can start their own butterfly gardens.

Please visit our website to see how this book was created, learn more about the migration and how to help save the butterflies.

May the winds be with you, Scott

Whitney Simmons
Principal

Whitney was born in Cincinnati, Ohio. She is the third oldest of five children. As a child, her siblings and friends called her "The Witness" because she was extremely inquisitive, wanting to know everything she could about people and their habits. Growing up, she loved to play school with her younger sister and neighborhood friends. Somehow, she always managed to become the teacher! Whitney loved school and knew by the time she was in fifth grade that she wanted to be an educator. She especially appreciated her elementary principal and fifth-grade teacher who showed constant care and concern for the children they served. Whitney wanted to be like them when she grew up. Now, after 13 years of teaching, Whitney has become a principal to assist other teachers and share her passion for helping students reach their highest potential. When she is not in school, Whitney enjoys hanging out with her family and friends, watching movies, taking walks and cooking. She lives in Springfield Township. Whitney believes we get out of life what we put into it — so give it your all!

Suzanne Nall
Art Teacher

Suzanne has been teaching art at Parker Woods Montessori for 12 years. When she was a little girl, she and her mother wrote a book about a baby robin the Nall family had rescued and rehabilitated the summer of 1977. Suzanne was seven years old and did all of the illustrations for the book. It was that year she knew she wanted to be a veterinarian, an artist or a teacher. Today, Ms. Nall has two dogs, is an artist and a teacher! She lives in Mount Washington with her two daughters Clarisse and Mariel. Suzanne says, "We are doing important work at Parker Woods, and I feel honored to be a part of a school striving to make the world a better place."

Nuria R. López Ortega
Parent and Project Coordinator

Nuria is a native of Madrid, Spain, but has lived in the Northeast and the Midwest of the US for over 25 years. She teaches Spanish and Linguistics to college students. In her free time, she enjoys biking, reading, glasswork, walking and dancing. Once a year, Nuria and her son Julian make the trip across the Atlantic Ocean back to her hometown to spend time with their family, just like the Monarchs! Nuria looks forward to creating a beautiful butterfly garden so that the Monarchs can feed on their way to Mexico. Nuria became involved in the book project Mirabella The Monarch because the character in the book gives us a great lesson of determination, perseverance and self-discovery, and inspires our students for the great journeys of life.

Acknowledgments

There isn't enough space here to give everyone the praise they deserve. Everyone has gone beyond the call of duty to help turn dreams into reality and make the world a better place. I mean that literally! I guarantee next year there will be more monarch butterflies in Cincinnati, Ohio because of us. And I hope to see that influence spread even further. Whitney, Suzanne and Nuria were the key players in this project, but there have been dozens of anonymous volunteers behind the scenes. Here are few more pivotal roles:

- **Tommy Rueff**, Founder and Director of Happen Inc., a non-profit agency that brings families and communities together through creative activities and special events. Just like his mission statement says, Tommy connected me to the people in the community to make the book happen.

- **Jody Weber** is a proud Parker Woods Montessori parent and writer of the grant that funded copies of the books for all the kids to take home.

- The grant was provided by the **Greater Cincinnati Foundation** and **Learning Links**, a Grant for Kids Program for Schools.

- **Allyson Stone-Weil** is another proud parent that helped with many aspects like making bookmarks, organizing events and just fixing things.

- Finally, thanks to my biggest fan **Sara Williams**. This book wouldn't exist without her.

Person, Place or Thing Credits

Student	Grade	Thing
Anonymous		Chrysalis
Braylen Tucker	0	Alligator
Christian Agliata	2	Moon
Diamond Blye	3	Bird belly (an object that a butterfly is likely to encounter)
Fairshawn Huckleby	4	Cars, trucks, humans
Jeremy Johnson	0	Butterfly Land
Julia E.	0	Baby rooster
Liam Brumfield	0	Snow
Lily Cullins	0	"Around the world"
Lucy Wales, Ramik Bell	2	Wall
Reuben Whitehead	3	"To the ends of the Earth"
Rokhaya Diaw	3	School
Saviogn Griffin	2	Spaceship
Sophia Banes	3	Pollen

Character Name Credits

Student	Grade	Name
Anonymous, Eboni Walker (3), Mariam Elwafi (2)		Bella the Butterfly (Inspiration for the title)
Amaya Soper	0	Flame the Horse
Anonymous		Butter the Fly
Ashanti Trimble	6	Bubbles the Bumble Bee
Benjamin Meyer	0	Crawley the Earthworm
Briana Moore	0	Blossom the Bird
Chris Upshaw	0	Waterspout the Spider
Danni Proctor	4	Cupcake the Dog
Devyn R. Moorefield	4	Hopper the Grasshopper
Dylan Moore	2	Cheese Puff the Pig
Faith Hamzy	0	Cenny the Centipede
Jemma Paul	4	Lily the Ladybug
Joey Kitchell	4	Dash the Snail
Miles Asselin	3	Tuck the Turtle
Obadiah	5	Ronaldo the Rooster
Rokhaya Kane	2	Cutey the Toad
Vivian Ward	0	Snowflake the Kitty

About the Character Creation and Illustrations

The book was truly a collaborative process. We had about 2100 characters and places, 1600 names and 520 drawings. There were hundreds of duplicate entries, which I think was a result of some great classroom discussions, but made it impossible to give credit to most entries like a *flower*. I spent about two weeks sorting everything: looking for permission slips, excluding bizarre suggestions or rewriting the story to match. We couldn't fit all the incredible ideas and pictures in the book; nonetheless, I'm very proud of the result—I believe it is a book to be cherished for a lifetime.

Illustration Credits

Illustration Credits

Illustration Credits

Honorable Mentions

Kindergarten • *Aiden Brauch, Aleciana Clark-Gaines, Alonzo Ellis, Althea Davis, Annie Kate Sayre, Anonymous, Coen Dwertman, Daishon Showes, Elliott Parran, Henry Wales, James Murphy V, Joaquín Alcántara, Kaydence, Keivais Wallington, Lamonnie Riley, Landon Hughes, London Strong, Madison Lampkin, Madison Wroblewski, Natalia Chenault, Nicholas Kramer, Noah Lagdameo, Odell B., Oliver Taylor, Payton Proctor, Raquell Rice, Ruby Solomon, Seneca Steinert, Tailor Williams, Weston Curriergroh, Wyatt Irwin, Zoe Caudill.*

First Grade • *Alexander Deitzel, Alice Appel, Anonymous, August W. Brown, Daphne Maxfield, Deontai Ellis, Elka Bender, Emma Bridgman-George, Fay'Onna Lewis, Gabrielle Wroblewski, Gloria Senga, Hugh Moothart, Jaedyn Hindsman, Jaylin Hill, Josephine Grider, Josiah Hensley, Kayllie Mayfield, Kellan Maskew, Kemper Jenkins, LeAaron Adamore, Mirabelle, Moya Patton, Na'Riyah H., Paytience Campbell, Sophia Strunk, Trinity Saffron, Victoria Strunk.*

Second Grade • *Adah Mosher, Aiden E., Anonymous, Brooklin E., Harmony Jackson, Jaelynn, Jerzy Quinn, Kayden, Kayla Miller, Rylei J. Fellows, Sebastian T., Serenity Briggerman, Zariah Clark*

Third Grade • *Anna Collins, Annika Daniels, Anonymous, Charlotte Solomon, Clark Sayre, Dacia Thompson, Ellie Maxfield, Gwen Sofia Agliata, Ian Reed, Ivy Hendricks, Jaden Crawford, Ke'ziaha Longmire, Syris Doughty, Tristan Maskew, Vaughn Froehlich, Zainab Dia, Zamar O. Deering.*

Fourth Grade • *Anonymous, David Huckleby, Ge'Nya Owens, Jada Martin-Showes, Jesiah L. Smith, Kendall Johnson, Lucjan Grider, Nate Morgan, Summer Jackson, Thalia H., Zao Lamb.*

Fifth Grade • *Alivia N. James, Alona Cunningham, Ananiah Marion, Anonymous, Brenden Maxfield, Cheyenne B., Emir Wheeler, Evan Robert Beem, Jade Crocheron, Joshäwneé Jones, Jullian Royal, Shantez Roberts Jr., Tianna Hill, Tiara Thomas, Tyrus Grant.*

Sixth Grade • *Ami Sangare, Anonymous, Elijah Kenny, Emily H. Kern, London Graham, Ni Jasia Monroe, Samarah Ross, Santino Daniels.*

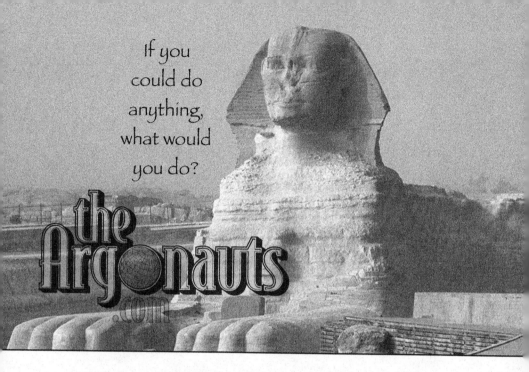

If you
could do
anything,
what would
you do?

the Argonauts .com

Make a Book and More Fun Online

~ Visit our website to help **Save the Butterflies**:
http://theArgonauts.com/save-the-butterflies/

~ Kids, **Submit Drawings Online** for the next book. Or parents, bring the **Make-A-Book Project** to your school with Scott's author-in-residence program.
http://theArgonauts.com/make-a-book-project/

~ Find **More Books** in this series:

- *Falling Uphill: Children's Edition,* the true story about Scott's bicycle ride around the world seeking happiness, and the Spanish edition, *Cayendo Hacia Arriba* illustrated by children in Argentina; this book was sponsored by the U.S. Department of State, and Scott was their Cultural Ambassador to Argentina.

- *Ruby the Red Worm's Dirty Job*

- *The Cupcake Boy*

- Order books signed by the author. (Bulk discounts available.)

~ Schedule Scott for **Speaking** events and workshops.

~ **Share** your inspirational stories on our website or Facebook Page:
https://www.facebook.com/FallingUphill/

~ Read about Scott's latest **Adventures** and news of upcoming books.

~ And much more of course...

CPSIA information can be obtained
at www.ICGtesting.com
Printed in the USA
FSOW04n0043280417
33501FS